Play Ball, Amelia Bedelia

by Peggy Parish

Pictures by Wallace Tripp

SCHOLASTIC INC.
New York Toronto London Auckland Sydney

ISBN 0-590-06203-4

50 49 48   2 3 4

Printed in the U.S.A.   23

for Jamie Murphy,
one of my favorite young friends,
with love

Amelia Bedelia walked by
the baseball field.
The Grizzlies team was there.

"I never saw such gloomy faces,"
said Amelia Bedelia.
"Did something terrible happen?"

"We play the Tornados today,"
said Jimmy.
"And Donny has the measles."

"There is no one
to take his place," said Tom.

"What about me?" said Amelia Bedelia.

"You!" said the boys. "Great!"

"But I don't know much
about the game," said Amelia Bedelia.

"I will explain it to you," said Tom.
"The idea of the game
is to hit the ball
and run to each of the bases.

8

The other team tries to get the ball
and tag you out," he said.

"That is easy enough,"
said Amelia Bedelia.

"Maybe we should warm her up
at bat," said Bob.

"Good idea," said Tom.
"Amelia Bedelia, you hit the ball
when Bob throws it."

"All right," she said.

Bob pitched the ball,
but Amelia Bedelia missed it.

"No, no," said Tom.
"You must step in
to meet the ball."

Bob pitched the ball again.

And Amelia Bedelia stepped in
to meet it.
"Ouch!" she said. "This game hurts!"

The boys taught Amelia Bedelia
how to bat.

Later she said, "All right,
I'm warmed up. In fact, I am hot."

"Then be here at two o'clock,"
said Jimmy. "The game starts then."

Amelia Bedelia went home.
She went right up to the attic.
"I know there is a uniform here,"
said Amelia Bedelia.
And there was one.

She took a nip here and a tuck there.
Soon that uniform was just right.

"That's done," said Amelia Bedelia.
"Now what should I do
until it is time to go?"

Then she saw the cookie jar.
"It's empty!" she said.
"Well, I will soon fix that."

Amelia Bedelia put some of this
and a bit of that into a bowl.
Amelia Bedelia mixed and she rolled.
Soon her cookies were all baked.

"There now," she said.
"That's done."

Amelia Bedelia looked at the clock.
"My goodness!" she said.
"I better be on my way."
Amelia Bedelia got her things
and went to the ball park.

"Here she is!
Here's Amelia Bedelia!"
called the Grizzlies.

"Then let's play ball,"
said the Tornados.

"The Tornados are up first,"
said Tom.
"Amelia Bedelia, you stand here.
Catch the ball if it comes your way."

"All right," she said.

"Batter up!" called the pitcher.
The pitcher threw the ball.
The batter hit it.
He ran to first base.

"Get the ball, Amelia Bedelia,"
yelled Tom. "Tag Jack
before he gets to second base."

"I must have a tag in here
somewhere," said Amelia Bedelia.
She tagged Jack.

Another boy came up to bat.

He hit the ball.

The ball landed near Amelia Bedelia.

"Throw it to first base,"
yelled the boys. "Put Dick out."

So Amelia Bedelia threw the ball
to first base.

Then she ran and grabbed Dick.
"How far out do you want him?"
she called.

"Amelia Bedelia!" shouted the boys.
"Put him down."

So Amelia Bedelia put Dick down.
"You sure do change your minds fast,"
she said. "You told me
to put him out!"

Dick got back on first base.
And the game went on.
The next batter missed the ball.
The catcher threw the ball
to the pitcher.
The pitcher missed it.

But Amelia Bedelia caught it!

"Hurry, Amelia Bedelia!
Throw the ball!" shouted the boys.
"Dick is trying
to steal second base."

"Steal second base!"
said Amelia Bedelia.
"That's not nice."

Amelia Bedelia ran
and picked up second base.
"It's all right now, fellows,"
she called. "Second base is safe."

"For gosh sakes, Amelia Bedelia!"
said the boys. "Put that back."

Amelia Bedelia looked puzzled.
"But he was going to steal it,"
she said.

"It's all right to steal bases,"
said Tom.
"That is part of the game."

"Oh," said Amelia Bedelia.

Finally the Tornados were out.
They had made two runs.
It was the Grizzlies' turn at bat.

Tom was first.
He struck out.

Then Jimmy had his turn.
He hit that ball hard.
He made it to third base.

Next it was Bob's turn.
He hit the ball.

"Pop fly," called the pitcher.
"I've got it."

"Pop fly?" said Amelia Bedelia.
"I didn't hear anything pop!"

Then it was Amelia Bedelia's turn.
"Come on, Amelia Bedelia," said Bob.
"Make a base hit
so Jimmy can come in."

"Which base should I hit?" she asked.

Tom said, "Just hit that ball
and run to first base!"

"All right," said Amelia Bedelia.
And that is just what she did.

Jimmy scored for the Grizzlies.
The team cheered.
The next player struck out.
The Tornados were at bat again.
The score was
Tornados 2, Grizzlies 1.
The Grizzlies called a time-out.

"Amelia Bedelia is not very good
in the field," said Jimmy.

"She gets all mixed up," said Tom.

"Maybe she could be catcher,"
said Bob.

The boys turned to Amelia Bedelia.
"You be the catcher," said Jimmy.

"What do I do?" she asked.

"Stand behind the batter
and catch the ball," said Jimmy.
"Then throw it back to the pitcher."

So Amelia Bedelia
stood behind the batter.
The pitcher threw the ball.
The batter was about to hit it.
But Amelia Bedelia pushed him
out of the way.

And Amelia Bedelia caught the ball.
"I got it, fellows!" she called.

The whole team groaned.
The Tornados were very angry.

"Put her someplace else,"
they shouted. "Put her way out."

So the Grizzlies put Amelia Bedelia
way out in the field.

The game was not going well
for the Grizzlies.
The score was
Tornados 8, Grizzlies 5.
The Grizzlies were at bat.
It was the last inning.

They had two outs.
The bases were loaded.
And Amelia Bedelia was at bat.
The Grizzlies were worried.

"Please, Amelia Bedelia," they said.
"Please hit that ball hard."

Amelia Bedelia
swung at the first ball.
She missed.

She swung at the second ball.
And again she missed.

"Please, Amelia Bedelia, please,"
shouted the Grizzlies.

Amelia Bedelia
swung at the next ball.
And oh, how she hit that ball!

51

"Run, Amelia Bedelia, run!"
yelled the boys.
"Run to first base."

And Amelia Bedelia ran.
"Tom says stealing
is all right," she said,
"so I'll just steal all the bases.
I will make sure the Grizzlies win."

Amelia Bedelia
scooped up first base,
and second base,
and third base.

"Home!" shouted the boys.
"Run home, Amelia Bedelia!"

Amelia Bedelia looked puzzled,
but she did not stop running.
And on her way she scooped up
home plate too.

The boys were too surprised
to say a thing.
Then Tom yelled, "We won!
We won the game!"

"Amelia Bedelia, come back!"
shouted the boys. "We won!"
But Amelia Bedelia was running
too fast to hear.
She did not stop
until she reached home.

"That is a silly game," she said.
"Having me run all the way home!"

Suddenly she heard a loud roar.
"Hurray! Hurray!
Hurray for Amelia Bedelia!"
There were the Grizzlies.
"We won! The score was
Grizzlies 9, Tornados 8,"
said Jimmy.
"You saved the game,
Amelia Bedelia."

"I'm glad I could help you boys out,"
said Amelia Bedelia.

"Maybe we should keep
Amelia Bedelia
on our team," said Bob.
"She could be our scorekeeper."

"I would be happy to keep
your score," said Amelia Bedelia.

"I have a nice box with a lock on it.
Your score would be safe with me."

The boys laughed.
"You will never learn baseball,"
said Tom. "Now can we please have
our bases and home plate back?"

"You sure can," said Amelia Bedelia.

Amelia Bedelia went inside.
She looked at home plate.
"Now what kind of a home
would use a plate like that?"
she said.
"But it isn't polite
to return an empty plate.
I will have to do something."

Amelia Bedelia looked at the cookies.
"That's it," she said.
Amelia Bedelia piled
home plate with cookies.
"Here you are, fellows," she said.

The boys quickly emptied
home plate.
"Those are the best cookies
I ever ate," said Jimmy.

"Maybe Amelia Bedelia will never
learn baseball," said Tom,
"but she sure can cook."

"Hurray for Amelia Bedelia!
Hurray for her cookies!"
shouted the boys.
Then the boys went on their way.

And Amelia Bedelia
went in to bake.
That cookie jar
was empty again!